Sammy Gets a Ride

written by
Karen Evans and Kathleen Urmston
illustrated by
Gloria Gedeon

KAEDEN ♥ BOOKS™

2

Mom came in the door and Sammy went out.

"I'll get him," I yelled.

Sammy ran in circles.
I chased him.

"I'll get him," my sister yelled.

Sammy ran through the back yard. My sister chased him.

"I'll get him," my big brother yelled.

Sammy ran across the front
yard. My big brother chased him.

8   "I'll get him," Mom said.

She got into our car and left the car door open.

Sammy ran to the car and jumped inside.

Mom closed the door and gave Sammy a ride...

...into the garage.